BIG
BONES

Also by
AMANDA SWIFT

THE BOYS' CLUB

AMANDA SWIFT

BIG BONES

SIMON AND SCHUSTER

SIMON AND SCHUSTER

First published in Great Britain by Simon & Schuster UK Ltd, 2005
A Viacom company

1 3 5 7 9 10 8 6 4 2

Simon & Schuster UK Ltd
Africa House
64-78 Kingsway
London WC2B 6AH

A CIP catalogue record for this book is available from the British Library

ISBN 0 689 87547 9

Typeset by M Rules
Printed and bound in Great Britain by
Cox & Wyman Ltd, Reading, Berks

For Tommy and Danny

ONE

I've had to move the button on my games skirt.
I sewed it myself because I don't want Mum to
know. It's a tragedy: I've only had it a week. I
must've mushroomed. Actually, I don't know
why they say 'mushroomed' for getting fatter.
Mushrooms are only seventy calories a kilo
and I don't think I could eat a kilo of them. It'd
be more accurate to say I've 'biscuited',
because that's what I've done. Eaten loads and
loads of biscuits. I don't binge, because I don't
eat them all in one go. I leave at least a couple
of minutes in between.

I've moved the button and I've tried the
skirt on. It's much more comfortable, but now

that the button has moved, the overlap on the skirt is smaller and, if I move, which I have to now and then, the overlap flaps open and my leg is exposed. My legs are worse than my stomach. They're like tree trunks – and I'm not talking spindly silver birch, I'm talking thick, stumpy palm trees.

Then Mum came in without knocking. So annoying. Almost as annoying as when she knocks and doesn't come in at all. She was brandishing a clutch of photos. 'Charlie! Look at these!' she exclaimed.

'I'd rather not,' I muttered, looking down at the floor at the giant shadow of my stomach and legs.

'But they're of your birthday!' she exclaimed. 'There's Sarah – doesn't she look gorgeous? – and Hannah and Alice, laughing away...' She held them up like trump cards. 'And you!' She held me up. The lump card. 'Look at you!' I tried not to. 'You've really grown this year!'

'I know,' I agreed. 'I've had to move the button on my games skirt.'

'Great!'

'How is that great?'

'At least you haven't had to buy a new one.'

'Mum. Being fat is not funny.'

'I'm not joking and you're not fat. You've just got big bones.'

'I have not got big bones!' I retorted. 'If I had got big bones I'd be even fatter than I am. I've just got small bones and lots of fat.'

'Tea'll be ready in a minute,' she said. 'That'll cheer you up.'

'I'm not hungry.'

"Course you are. It's tea-time.'

She plonked the photos on my desk and went. I glanced at them – my best friend, Sarah, was wearing a fantastically skimpy top. My joint second-best friends, Alice and Hannah, were both wearing tiny trousers. Alice's were covered in badges. She's collected so many there's only a small patch on her bottom where there *aren't* any, which is just as well, otherwise it'd be pretty uncomfortable when she sits down. I was wearing a long thick cardigan that made me look like a small mammoth.

Mum burst back in. 'You've got lovely eyes.'

'Thanks,' I said, very sarcastically. 'They're the only bit of me that isn't fat.'

She went away again.

I looked at the photos again. I suppose my eyes *are* OK. They're kind of smiley, like the rest of my face when I'm in a good mood. I was in a good mood then because it was my birthday. I'd got a camera, so we went to the park and took a load of photos of ourselves – not because we're vain, more because it was freezing cold and we were the only people in the park.

'Tea's ready!'

Here we go.

Can you imagine an orange kitchen? Not orange in a modern, funky way, orange in a sad, old-fashioned way. When Gran went to India 'to think', she left us the house; Mum and Dad haven't done anything to it since so it's unfashionably out-of-fashion. The only good thing about orange is that it matches my brothers' hair, but unfortunately it doesn't make them disappear. Nothing does.

I was a very happy only child until I was six. I had no need for any siblings and then suddenly I got three. This was really unlucky because triplets are dead unusual these days. Maybe after me Mum's reproductive system decided it couldn't cope with another big fat egg, so it split the next one into three. The boys may *look* the same but they never want anything that's the same.

'No broccoli,' said Tom, as I walked into the kitchen.

'No potato,' said Perry.

'No meat,' said George.

Mum winced but doled out three plates of food, each with one thing missing.

'No meat,' said Tom.

'No broccoli,' said Perry.

'No potato,' said George.

'Swap,' said Mum.

A dangerous word to say to my brothers. They embarked on an elaborate exchange of food until they each still only had one thing on their plate, but more of it. Still, they didn't throw anything, so all in all it went well.

Mum sighed again: 'You've forgotten something.'

'Ketchup!' they cried, together.

'No. *Please*.'

'Ketchup, *please*,' they chanted.

'And thanks for the food,' mumbled Perry. He's the charmer. If you can call remembering to say 'thank you' once in a while charming.

'Yeah, thanks,' mumbled the other two, belligerently.

The front door opened. Dad came into the hall and sighed. We all sighed back. We've done that for ever. When we were little we thought it was his way of saying hello.

He came into the kitchen. 'Hi,' he said, weakly.

'Hi,' we all replied, weakly.

'Bad day?' asked Mum.

'Of course' said Dad, and sighed again as he sat down at the table. Dad's a complaints officer. He has to sit in an office all day and listen to people complaining, and he can't complain about it. Mum served him up a steaming plate of food to take his mind off it.

'Charlie?'

'Broccoli, please.'

'You can't just have broccoli.'

'George has.'

'*I* need it to make me grow,' George said proudly.

'And you mean I don't?' I responded sharply. 'Are you saying I'm fat?'

I shouldn't have said it. The triplets were on to it in a flash.

'Are you saying I'm fat?' they chanted. 'Are you saying I'm fat? Are you saying I'm fat?'

I stuck my legs out under the table and rattled them along their three pairs of grimy knees. The boys are still only six so I can get them without them always getting me back. So I do, as often as I can, while I still can.

'Boys!' said Mum and Dad in unison. 'You may go.'

This suited them because they'd actually finished the one thing they each ate, so they did a very strange thing: they did what they were told.

I stared at my broccoli. I didn't really feel

like eating it. I wanted meat and potatoes as well. Mum misunderstood and thought I didn't even want my broccoli.

'At least have that,' she pleaded.

'No,' I said. 'They've put me off.' I scraped back my chair, flung myself towards a standing position and stomped off upstairs.

When I got to my room I chucked myself on my bed, because that's what you do when you're upset. I didn't cry: I was too angry to cry. But what had made me so angry? The boys? Me? Potatoes, in all their forms? I calmed myself down by deciding I had to do something: lose it. Not my temper, the extra kilos. I'd had enough of being an elephant in a family of gazelles. A hippo in a class of cranes. I wanted to be an antelope in whatever the collective noun for antelopes is. I wanted to be as sleek, as fast, as beautiful as everyone else – or even more than everyone else, if I could manage it.

But how? I knew all about eating less and exercising more. I knew the calories in crispbread and the amount of butter in butter. I knew a big breakfast was better than a big tea and a small lunch was better than an hourly snack. I knew that being in a bad mood could make you eat too much; I knew that being in a good mood could make you eat too much; I knew that being bored could make you eat too much. So really there wasn't much time in between when you could eat a bit less. All this thinking about food had made me really hungry and, after all, I hadn't eaten my tea...

I crept downstairs to the kitchen. Luckily Mum and Dad had gone off to watch *The Simpsons*. It's the one thing we usually all enjoy doing together, apart from running a very complicated system of bets on when the boys' teeth are going to fall out. I could see a lovely plate of meat, potatoes and broccoli warm and waiting for me in the oven. I tucked into it while I flicked through one of my mum's magazines, hoping there'd be a diet that I could follow until I had a perfect body.

It was like one of those games where you have to pick up wooden sticks without disturbing any of the others, except that what I was doing was trying not to disturb Mum. I turned the pages ever so quietly but she still heard.

'You're not going on a diet!' she bellowed from the lounge, before I'd even got to the diet section.

'I'm not!' I screeched back, lying.

'Good,' she shouted back.

I did feel like crying now. Why wouldn't Mum let me do something that was good for me?

Then Mum came in. She sat on the chair next to me and talked quietly. She always does that when she's trying to be nice.

'I've told you before, Charlie, you've just got big bones.'

'Is *this* a bone?' I said, pinching my stomach. 'Is *this* a bone?' I said, pinching my arm.

'You'll shoot up.'

'Great,' I said, sarcastically. 'Then there'll be even more of me, so I'll be even fatter.'

'No,' she said, still quietly. 'Things'll sort themselves out.'

'I can't wait for that to happen,' I said, sternly.

'Well, you'll have to, because you shouldn't diet when you're not fully grown.'

'But I've already grown far too much, in the wrong places.'

'Have a drink and a yogurt,' she said, kindly, and she gave them to me to take upstairs.

Later, while I was doing my homework, I started thinking about the diet again. If Mum was going to make it difficult for me, then how could I do it? I could pretend I'd got a tummy bug. I wasn't sure she'd believe me. I could pretend I'd gone off biscuits, cakes, sweets, pies, crisps and nuts. I didn't think she'd believe that either. I could hide some of my food under my fork. Pathetic.

No. I would do it sensibly. I would simply cut down... and I would start with my yogurt. I wouldn't eat it. It was still sitting on my desk, waiting to be the treat at the end of my physics homework. Raspberry. My favourite.

No! I could do without it. But what could I do with it? If I put it back in the fridge,

Mum would notice. If I threw it in the bin, she would see. I would have to be clever – very clever – and luckily, for once, I was. I sneaked to the bathroom, poured the yogurt down the basin, rinsed the basin, nipped back into my room and threw the empty yogurt pot in my bin. I even swished the spoon around in it to make it look like it had been licked. Genius.

By the time I went to bed I felt thinner. I had managed not to eat my bedtime biscuit by slipping it into my dressing gown pocket and then crushing it into a pot plant. (It was chocolate and didn't show up against the earth.) So I'd probably saved about two hundred calories. If I did that every day I'd have lost a kilo by the end of the week, and if I lost a kilo every week... I drifted off with sweet dreams of the perfect me. I planned the clothes I'd buy, the parties I'd go to, the boyfriends I'd have...

And then I woke up. I never wake up in the night, except for when Perry has bad dreams and shouts 'CHICKENS!!' at the top of his voice, but otherwise I never wake up. Why had I woken up? It didn't take long for me to work it out: I was hungry. I was deprived. Someone had denied me my yogurt and my biscuit and, even though that someone was me, I had to get my own back.

I flung back the covers. I checked the time: 2.00 a.m. Even my late-night-telly-watching parents would be in bed by now. I crept out of my room, down the stairs and, of course, into the kitchen. I could have had a glass of water – an apple, a crispbread, maybe; but no, I went straight for the biscuit tin. I got out the biscuit I was owed from bedtime and, to make up for the loss, I got out four more. I shut the tin and raced upstairs, into my room and under the duvet. I ate them all without thinking or chewing until there were crumbs all over me and my bed. I carefully picked them up and ate them too. Then, as if this had never happened, I turned over and went to sleep. I didn't even brush my teeth. Now I was going to be toothless as well as fat.

TWO

Next day, Sarah and I met on the corner. We always do that. Our journey to school is precision-timed: Sarah and I meet at 8.05 and walk briskly up the avenue so that Hannah and Alice can meet us at the roundabout at 8.10; then we all walk on to school together.

Sarah's my best friend, even though she's thinner and prettier than I am. Usually people are best friends with people who have similar figures and faces. I suppose that's because most fat, ugly people don't want to be made to look worse by hanging out with much better-looking people. But I like Sarah too much to ditch her because she's thin. She's got lovely rosy cheeks and a shy smile and she always listens to me. I don't know why she's friends with me. She says it's because I'm funny and fun, but I can't really believe that.

I didn't think I'd have to tell Sarah about the skirt incident because I hadn't got it on. I thought I had at least until gym class in the afternoon, but she noticed immediately. Not the skirt, of course, because it was in my bag, but my mood.

'What's up?' she asked.

'Nothing,' I muttered.

'What kind of nothing?' she asked. She knows nothing is always something, of course.

'My games skirt—' I started, but she didn't give me time to finish.

'Oh, that!' she shrieked. 'Don't worry about that. If you've had to move the button you'll probably have to move it back in a week or two.'

Has she got CCTV cameras trained on my house? How did she know?

'I bet it looks better a bit looser...'

So she'd noticed. I had only just realised that I was slowly being severed in two by a piece of school uniform and she'd known for days.

'Yeah, but it isn't loose. My belly's just bounced out to fill the extra space.'

'Oh, I know what you mean.' No she doesn't. She's a size six. 'I've just gone up to a size eight.' OK, so she's a size eight.

'Oh my god!' I said, way ironically.

'I know,' she said, choosing not to get the irony. 'You've only had to move a button a bit, I had to go up a *whole* size.'

'Sarah, I'm already a size fourteen.'

'So? That's not so big. And anyway, they're just numbers.'

'Yeah, but some numbers are bigger than others.'

You can hear Hannah and Alice before you see them, because they're always laughing. It was the same today. I could understand it if I knew what they were laughing about, but it's always really ordinary things like: 'What d'you have for breakfast – same old cereal?' and then they really laugh, like it's a fantastic joke. I think I've got quite a good sense of humour, but I don't get their jokes. I used to find it a bit annoying but now I've decided that like some people cry easily, they laugh easily.

'Hi, cats,' they said and they both laughed.

'Hi,' we said and fell into step.

'Watch anything good last night?' asked Hannah.

'Yeah,' I said. 'Blank screen.'

'Any good?' asked Sarah, deadpan.

'Yeah,' I answered. 'Well, better than what was on.'

Then Sarah reached into her pocket. 'I saw this yesterday and thought you'd like it.' She handed Alice a badge which said: 'My other boyfriend's better.'

Nice one.

When we got to class, our teacher was waiting for us with a tin of biscuits. Miss Longbottom – yes, that *is* her name and why on earth she didn't change it the minute she became a teacher I have no idea. In fact, why didn't she change it the minute she was old enough to realise how funny it was? Anyway, we all really like her, despite the name and not just because she gives us biscuits.

Some of the boys have got a bit of a crush on her. They pretend they haven't, but it's obvious because they do things like flick up their gelled hair when she comes in the room. Total giveaway.

Miss Longbottom isn't just our form teacher, she's our German teacher as well. This of course means that German is my favourite subject. I don't know if it would be my favourite subject if she didn't teach it; it's hard to tell, because she brings in her guitar and teaches us songs, and does plays, and gives us homebaked German biscuits. Yum. I don't know if I'd like German if it didn't involve eating biscuits.

The only tragedy about German is that Sarah doesn't do it. She chose Spanish instead. I miss her in the classes but the biscuits make up for it. German's first on Monday morning, after lunch on Wednesday, and last on Friday, so it's a nice stepping stone through the week. Today, however, I thought all that was going to change. Sarah and the others who don't do German went off to Spanish and Miss Longbottom just stood there, with no guitar, no playbooks, no biscuits in her hand. This is it, I thought, that was all to entice us in, like the biscuit that gets the dog into the basket. Now that we've taken to German she's going to cut the treats and teach us the subjunctive.

How could I even have thought that mean thought about Miss Longbottom! She got a piece of paper out of her bag. Not very promising in itself, I admit, but then she started to read from it and I perked up no end.

'I've arranged for you to have some German email friends,' she said.

'How will they work out what we're writing?' asked David, always the first to see the negative in the situation.

'Because you'll write in German,' said Miss Longbottom, as severely as she could. Nearly everyone groaned.

'And how will we work out what *they're* writing?' queried Alfie, never the first to grasp anything.

'Because they will write in English,' said Miss Longbottom, wearily.

'Can't we just write in our own language and get you to translate it?' quipped Alice.

'No,' said our patient teacher, 'and don't try

it because I'll be checking print-outs of your emails to see how you're getting on.'

This brought on a wave of moaning and questions and general chat. Miss Longbottom let it go for a bit and then called us to attention by doing a piercing wolf-whistle.

'Right,' she said, getting out some sticky labels. 'Here are the names and addresses of your correspondents. If you don't have email at home you can book to use the computers in the library. Hannah, you have Erica; Alice, you have Barbara; David, you have Jürgen; Alfie, you have Hans…'

So she went on, right through the class, without mentioning me. What have I done? I thought, because usually she includes me a lot in class. Sarah says it's because she likes me, but I think it's because she thinks I'll fall asleep if she doesn't keep asking me questions. I thought she'd forgotten me until finally, last of all, she said: 'Charlie.' I looked at her as intensely as a kitten at an uncatchable bird. 'There's a slight mismatch in the classes, so you're going to have to write to a boy.'

Why did she have to say it out loud?

Everyone laughed and pointed and, worst of all, everyone knew. If she'd told me quietly I could have pretended it was a girl, but there it was, as boyish as a boy could be: Frank. Not Frankie. Frank, from Frankfurt. Not very promising. Why me? Because I've got three brothers? Because I'm so fat? This would make me end up even fatter because it was a totally stressful situation, even more stressful than when I had to play for the under-twelves netball team and my bra strap pinged open every time I shot at goal.

At the end of class I stormed out before anyone could talk to me. I told Sarah about it at morning break.

'What's the problem?' she asked, choosing to ignore the obvious one.

'I don't particularly get on with English boys, so why should I get on with a German one?'

'You don't have to get *on* with him, you just have to write to him.'

'Yes, but then everyone will think we've got a thing going.'

'Just tell them you haven't.'

'What if I have?'

'Tell them you haven't.'

'What if I haven't?'

'Tell them you have.'

For once, she couldn't calm me down. I had to resort to a currant bun, a chocolate biscuit and a can of fizzy drink. They succeeded in taking my mind off it for a while because they made me feel sick.

THREE

I wasn't going to tell Mum about it. I wasn't going to tell Dad about it. I certainly wasn't going to tell the boys about it. Then Miss Longbottom sent a letter home about it and so they all found out about it anyway. I tried to get Mum to complain and say I had to have a girl to write to, but she wouldn't.

'It'll do you good.'

'In what way could it possibly do me good to write to some stupid German boy?'

'Don't be racist.'

'I'm not being racist. I wouldn't want to write to a stupid French boy, or a stupid Spanish boy, or a stupid Nepalese boy. It's the fact he's a boy I object to, not that he's foreign.'

'He might like football,' piped Perry. We were eating tea at the time so unfortunately the whole family was there, sticking its collective nose in my business.

'Exactly,' I spat.

'I had a French penfriend when I was a lad,' said Dad, dreamily. 'He loved football and we wrote to each other about it all the time. I learnt the French words for "whistle" and "indirect free kick".'

Even Mum glared at him for that unhelpful remark. Then she started on me.

'Charlie, you're twelve years old, there's nothing wrong with you corresponding with a boy.'

'There's nothing right about it, either,' I riposted. I like to have the last word, even if I've actually lost the argument.

Next day I asked Miss Longbottom to swap me with someone else but she said I was best suited to Frank. I knew what she really meant was that I was so fat there was no danger of him falling for me.

There was no escape. It was homework, after all, and if I didn't do it I'd get detention, and that meant missing the daily school homecoming biscuit tin raid. So I reluctantly turned on the computer and wrote to him. This is what I wrote, although of course it was in German. I'm not writing all the German out because anyone who doesn't do German wouldn't be able to understand it. Nor would anyone who *does* do German, because I'm sure it was full of mistakes.

From: Charlie
Sent: 15 January 5.06 p.m.
To: Frank
Subject: Email friend

Dear Frank
Do you say 'dear' in German? Obviously you're not my dear. Hello. I think you say that in German. My name is Charlie. It's a boy's name. My real name is Charlotte but everyone calls me Charlie.
I'm 12. I live in Crystal Palace, a London suburb. 150 years ago there was a glass

palace here but there was a fire and it
burnt down.
My father works in an office, my mother
doesn't work. I've got three brothers:
triplets, 6 years old. Unfortunately.
I can't write any more. I've got other
things to do.
Bye, Charlie

There. Done. I sent it and ticked it off in my
homework book. I didn't think any more about
it and got on with my art homework: a picture
of the Great Exhibition at Crystal Palace. I
drew an elephant – something bigger than me
for a change.

Before I turned the computer off I checked to
see if any emails had arrived in the last fifty-two
minutes. I didn't know who I thought would
have written, when only five people have my
address. I'm always hoping someone will have
given it to a film star and he'll have written to
me because he wants to get to know me better.

There was a mail! A mail from Frank. I
couldn't stop myself being a bit excited,
especially when I read it.

From: Frank
Sent: 15 January 5.59 p.m.
To: Charlie
Subject: Femail friend

Dear Charlie
Thanks for your short but interesting
letter.
It is good that you learn the German,
although here all speak the English,
although not very well, as you see from
this! To me it is no surprise that I am not
your dear, because we have not ever
met. Also, I am not an animal with
antlers.
So, you live in a big glass house, yes? Are
you like a tomato or a palm tree? Sorry,
silly joke. I live in an apartment on the
third floor with my parents and a sister.
Oh, and our dog also. I am 13. The
apartment is in a small town which is
really now part of Frankfurt, but on the
edge. My father is I think you call it a park
ranger. My mother teaches people to
swim, children mostly but adults too. My

sister is 10 and sometimes very annoying,
maybe not as bad as triplets. My sister is
madly on our dog, Schiller, but Schiller is
madly on football, as I. I am a fan of
Eintracht Frankfurt, have you heard of it?
It is the big club in Frankfurt – do you like
football? Crystal Palace is a football team,
too, no? The ball must often break the
windows (sorry again).
My hobbies are reading: thriller novels but
others too. And cooking – yes, a boy
cooking! – I want to do it as a job when I
leave the school. And also going to
cinemas and photography and travel. One
day hopefully I come to London, it is a
very exciting city I hear. Much better than
Frankfurt.
Time to go. Hopefully you are well and
maybe write back to me soon some time.
Tschüss (is what we say for 'goodbye' to
friends)
Frank (short for 'Frankenstein' – no not
actually!)

I was totally speechless, even though I was on

my own and I don't normally talk to myself anyway. He sounded nice! I'd never actually imagined he'd be nice. Maybe it was because I didn't have to talk to him or look at him, so he didn't remind me of all the scruffy boys at school. We only had words between us and that made it much more like talking to a girl – although I was well aware even from one mail that he was clearly not a girl, but I didn't mind. I wrote back straight away, but didn't send it until the next morning because I thought that if I replied immediately it would look a bit uncool, which was totally how I felt.

From: Charlie
Sent: 16 January 8.00 a.m.
To: Frank
Subject: Malefriend

Hello Frank. Thank you for your nice letter. Sorry that my letter was a bit short. I thought you would be boring but you're not.
I'm glad you like cooking. Can you make German biscuits? I really like them. I can make English biscuits called gingerbread men. They

look like my brothers. I love eating them.

I really like films but I don't go often. I get videos out a lot. Do you?

I don't know Eintracht Frankfurt. I don't like football much but my father and brothers go to Crystal Palace. There's also a park called Crystal Palace, with a big swimming pool and an athletics track and dinosaurs. I really like them.

Yes, London is exciting. Sometimes a bit too exciting. You never know if you're going to get home without any 'excitement', that's to say, without your mobile phone or your purse.

Do you eat frankfurters, Frankenstein?

Until next time,

Bye, Charlie

When I got back from school, there was this waiting for me:

From: Frank
Sent: 16 January 4.08 p.m.
To: Glass Palace Girl
Subject: I am not a sausage

Hi Charlie

Your German is very good, but in one
place it sounds funny, as you say, 'I like
eating my brothers'. Lucky there is so
many. Maybe some time we swap biscuits.
Or maybe you have the German biscuits
and I eat your brothers. OK, only one.
Yes, videos more than cinema, it is
perhaps lazy but cheaper also. And of
course you can play back and watch again
and again the parts you really like. Or the
parts you did not hear well enough.
American accents are easier than UK, but I
like the UK accents better. This little town
where I live (not Frankfurt) is boring
boring but at least it gives a very good
video store where they have almost all the
old great films, as well as the new ones.
I have to say I think your district of
London sounds a bit crazy. First a big glass
house with no plants. Then a football club
that is named a glass house and nobody
knows where it belongs. And now a park
with people swimming and running and
dinosaurs ambling about. What the hell is

going on with this place? Maybe it is the next in the *Jurassic Park* series of films. It sounds fun, even if you invent it.

I formally announce that the people of Frankfurt never accept that this sausage you call 'Frankfurter' is from our city. We call it a 'Wiener', so it is the people of Vienna you must blame. Announcement ended.

Write back when you can.

Tschüss

We were off. We wrote most days, sometimes more than once, sometimes more than twice, and once, when we were exchanging favourite jokes, forty-nine times. We didn't just write about fun subjects, though – we discussed rainforests, smoking, parents, education, and what is the ideal length for trousers.

We just seemed to click – like old friends, except we had the excitement of being new friends. I can't deny that Frank being a boy made it special, too. It wasn't that we flirted, but I certainly now felt that we were the lucky ones. I had thought that having a boy would be so much worse, but it turned out so much better.

When I talked to Alice and Hannah about their German correspondents I decided I was the best off. Alice had Barbara, who liked knitting and had knitted her a badge in the shape of a rabbit – I didn't think she'd be wearing that one to go out. Hannah had Erica, who'd told her about a new TV channel that only plays music by boys who shout. I could live without that knowledge.

I didn't talk too much about Frank. I didn't want anything to spoil it. I played it down, like it wasn't too great, although sometimes I wanted to scream to the chimney pots: 'I'VE GOT A BOYFRIEND AND I LOVE HIM!!!!' That wouldn't have been entirely true, either. He wasn't my boyfriend; I didn't love him; but I did feel all warm and tickly inside when I read his mails.

Like a rollercoaster, the lows only come after the highs, so I guess I was heading for one. It came the next morning, in the form of a letter for me from Germany. At first I was pleased: I could see from the postmark that it was from Frankfurt, so must be from Frank. I'd given him my address before, when he'd wanted to send me some biscuits for answering his questionnaire: Fifty Things You Should Know About Me. Luckily one of the questions wasn't about my weight.

I never thought about what might be in the envelope, not even biscuits – I just ripped it open. Inside was a photo, the most amazing I've ever seen. It was of Frank.

FOUR

It wasn't that he was so good-looking. It's just
that he was looking straight at me. OK, you
may say, but he'd be looking straight at anyone
who was looking at the photo – but I didn't
think it worked like that. I even did an
experiment. I went up to Tom (not because I
actually wanted to, but because he was the
only person around: Mum was in the shower;
George and Perry were fighting over those
gifts they give you to fight over in cereal
packets) and I held the photo up right in front
of his face. 'Do you think he's looking at you?'
I demanded.

'No,' said Tom.

See. I was right. He was looking at me, not Tom. And then Tom spoilt it.

'He's looking at whoever's taking the photo.'

Trust Tom to give with one comment and take away with the next. I went up to my room with the photo so no one would disagree with me.

I don't know what it was about Frank. He was wearing boy uniform: baggy black T-shirt and baggy black trousers. He had interesting green eyes; he had impressive black hair. He had a few silly freckles. But most of all he looked friendly, like he already knew me. Well, I suppose he did, a bit, but not as well as I felt I now knew him.

I tore off the stamp because I'm collecting them for the hedgehog sanctuary. As I tore, I saw something which changed my mood completely. I realised, once I felt down, that I'd been feeling quite up; but that was all over now. *'Send me also your photo please. Here is my address'* was written in a boyish scrawl on the back. Nothing lasts. What on earth could I do now? I could pretend I hadn't seen the request.

After all, some people tear open letters without ever looking at the back of the envelope... Hmm. I didn't quite believe that. And anyway, if I did pretend I hadn't seen it, he'd probably ask again, and then he might think there was some kind of issue about me sending a photo – which of course there was, so that was no good.

It wasn't that I wanted him to think I was dead pretty, or fancy me, or anything; it's just I didn't want him to know what I actually looked like. Actually, it was worse than that: *I* didn't want to know what I looked like. I didn't want to have to face up to it.

I was a bit quiet on the way to school. The only trouble with having really good friends is that they know you so well they notice the tiniest change in your behaviour, like the fact that usually I'm full of news and views and jokes and chat, and today I was a bit quiet. Sarah noticed immediately. 'You're a bit quiet,' she said.

'Yes,' I said, a bit weakly. 'I didn't have any breakfast.'

'No!' she gasped, because she knows I

always have breakfast, even when it's not breakfast-time.

'I'm feeling a bit nervous,' I said, knowing she'd ask me why.

'Why?' she asked.

'Frank has sent me his photo,' I said, reaching into my pocket.

'Show me show me show me!' she demanded, practically ripping it out of my hand.

'Careful,' I said.

'Wow!' she said.

'He's not *that* good-looking.'

'I know,' she said, 'but he looks really nice. Your type.'

My type? How does she know he's 'my type'? I'm only twelve. I haven't had a boyfriend yet – unless you count David, who I kiss-chased when I was four.

'You're not nervous,' she said knowingly. 'You're in love.'

Thank goodness, Hannah and Alice joined us then and I didn't have to talk about it any more. Sarah insisted on showing them the photo, but I just let them be impressed and

40

kept quiet. They also thought I was in love. Was I? I think it was more like shock; shock and disappointment. Shock that he was so cute, disappointment that he'd never fall for a lump like me.

I decided that I would decide what to do about the photo after school while I was doing my homework, which that day was french, geography and citizenship. I made a pile, like I always do, with my schoolbooks on the left of my desk. I put each book in front of me when I'm working on it and to the right when I've finished. I slipped the photo between geography and citizenship, as if dealing with it were as simple as doing a graph of rainfall, or deciding what to do if you see someone lying down in the road. But when I got to the photo it was just as complicated. There he was, looking at me again.

Well, I would look back at him. What was the problem with that? I'd send him a photo of me, maybe one of the recent ones of my birthday. There, I'd decided. I picked up the photo and put it on the right-hand pile, to show it was dealt with. But then, instead of picking up my citizenship exercise book, I picked the photo up again and put it back in front of me. Clearly I hadn't decided anything at all.

After my homework I had a bath to relax, but it made me feel worse because I was thinking about the photo all the time. When I came back from the bathroom, Mum was in my room.

'Do you *have* to come in here?' I said, with reprimand in my voice.

'Yes,' she said, 'until you teach your clothes to walk upstairs.'

There was a basket of clean washing at her feet. It's true I'm not great about irrelevant little things like helping Mum.

She picked up Frank's photo. 'He looks nice,' she said, clutching it in her mitt. 'You *must* send one back.'

I didn't answer, partly because I knew what she was going to say next.

'How about one of your birthday? They're so good of you.'

'Yes, I will,' I said, just to get rid of her.

'Good,' she said. 'Do you need a stamp?'

'NO!!!' I shrieked, completely overreacting.

I have to admit my mum knows just how to react when I'm overreacting. She under-reacts to balance me out. This time she slipped out of the door, pausing only to straighten my duvet.

I knew what I had to do. Sighing heavily, I got out the photos of my birthday. I flicked through, looking for me, hoping that by magic I would have changed into someone else. But no, there I was, my tummy still sticking out from my mammoth cardigan. I so wished it wasn't me.

Why did it matter? Frank and I already got on. It wasn't like knowing what I looked like was going to make him feel sick and stop him writing to me – although I wouldn't blame him if it did. I suppose I felt cornered. I had never lied about what I looked like, but I had never told him either. I was just a floating voice, arriving in print on his screen. That was rather a nice feeling. But from the moment he got this photo, I was pinned down. I was me: the voice of the body, the body of the voice. He would associate everything he read with the fat girl in the photo and my identity would be pinned down and immutable.

There was no escape. I found an envelope and stuffed the photo in. Now my photo was almost on its way to Germany. The one underneath was the lovely one of Sarah, smiling and skinny. I didn't even think about what I did next, I just did it. I whipped my photo out of the envelope and put Sarah's in instead.

Then I went straight downstairs to ask Mum for a stamp; but Mum being Mum she would never do anything as simple as just *give* me a stamp. 'What's it for?... Is it for that photo?... It might weigh more than the standard rate – and anyway it's for Germany, so you'll have to go to the post office...' And so on.

I could do all that tomorrow. As I got ready for bed, I kept finding myself looking at the envelope. Even as I was dropping off to sleep, it was in sight. Needless to say, I dreamt about it. It was a nightmare. Sarah found out and never spoke to me again and Frank found out and never wrote to me again. As I slowly woke up, my first thought was to take the photo of Sarah out of the envelope, put in one of me, and face the music – although I didn't really know where music came into it, unless I was then going to spend my life listening to sad songs.

I opened my eyes and put my hand out for the envelope, but it wasn't there. I looked on the floor, in my bag, on the ceiling. Mad, I know, but I had a hairband stuck up there for a long time. My mind raced to the usual suspects and I flew down the stairs into the lounge and launched myself across their knees. They were sitting calmly in a line on the sofa watching telly, so this acrobatic feat was technically possible, although a little ungainly.

'Where's my letter?'

'What letter?' said George, innocently.

Obviously my brothers are known for claiming their innocence, but George's complete disinterest and vacant look tempted me to believe him. As did Perry's remark: 'What *is* a letter anyway?'

'It's that bit of paper for Grandma Mum

writes in wobbly handwriting and then you sign,' muttered Tom.

I heaved myself off the sofa and went in search of my next suspect. She was in the kitchen, washing potatoes. I opened my interrogation: 'Where's my letter?'

'In the letterbox.'

'Which one?'

'It's all right, I had to go to the post office so I got the right stamp for it.'

'I don't care about the stamp!' I exploded.

'Well, you should. There's a fine on unpaid postage now, and some people don't bother and so they never get their mail.'

'I hope they *do* never get it.'

'Well, why did you send it?'

'I didn't send it, *you* did!'

She actually paused and turned round, letting water drip on the floor. 'Didn't you want it sent?'

There. She'd cornered me. I didn't want to admit that I'd not only sent a photo of Sarah but I'd now changed my mind and wanted to send one of me. I avoided this situation by shuffling out of the room. She turned back to her potatoes and said that classic mother thing: 'I was only trying to help.'

I picked up a banana as I left.

'You forgot to seal it,' she called after me. 'I did that for you too.'

Thanks a bunch, Mum.

FIVE

'I have a complaint,' I said to Dad as he was pulling on his Palace socks. He always goes to the match in full kit. I think he hopes against hope that they'll pull him on as a substitute.

'It's Saturday, Charlie,' said Dad wearily. 'I don't do complaints on Saturday.'

'But I've got a complaint on a Saturday,' I continued, 'and you haven't got time for my complaints the rest of the week.'

'OK, then, complain away.'

'It's Mum,' I said.

'Oh,' he said wearily. 'Mum again.'

'Yes.'

'What's she done this time?'

'She posted my letter,' I said, full of self-righteousness.

'Oh,' said Dad. 'Didn't you want it posted?'

'Kind of,' I replied. I was faltering a bit now.

'Did she put on the wrong stamp?' asked Dad.

'No,' I admitted.

'Did she charge you for transport?'

'No,' I confessed, 'but that was only because she walked.'

'She could have charged you wear and tear on her shoes,' said Dad.

Whose side was he on? The right side, I guess. That's why he's good at his job. I realised my cause for complaint was slipping between my fingers. Not that my mum was slipping between my fingers because she was out at Asda, but the whole case, which I'd brought to Dad in the vain hope that he could do something about it.

'So Mum posted your letter for you,' said Dad, going over the facts. 'I can't see the problem with that.'

Of course there was no problem, not with that. I couldn't tell him that the problem was not with the posting of the envelope, it was with the posting of what was *inside* the envelope.

'You see I posted a photo of Sarah to a boy I've never met because I'm too embarrassed of what I look like to send a photo of me.' How could I say that to Dad? I couldn't and I didn't. It was too intimate, like bras.

I decided I had to deal with this myself. I headed upstairs past the boys, who were using the washing basket as a round-the-world yacht. That works quite well, but the landing isn't quite as good as the Atlantic. It doesn't really *flow*.

I didn't get involved with their game because I had my mission in mind. Sometimes I pause to provide a bit of wind or an enemy attack, but today I marched straight into my bedroom and logged on.

From:	Charlie
Sent:	15 Feb 10.34 a.m.
To:	Frank
Subject:	Photo

Hi. Sorry, I sent you the wrong photo.
You've got a photo of my best friend
Sarah. I'll send you one of me instead.

There. I'd told him. And I'd been really mature and not gone into all the reasons why I'd done it. I didn't think he'd want to know about that. *I* didn't really want to know about that, so why should he? In any case, I find with boys generally they're not so really interested in the story that leads up to the whole point of the story. In fact they look a bit blank, like a turned-off television, while you're doing the lead-up, and then they suddenly switch on when you get to the end. Whereas when I'm talking to my girl friends, they like the lead-up almost more than the ending. In fact we often don't get to the end of stories because we get so involved in the beginning and the middle.

So, the mail was done. I moved the cursor up to SEND and then, almost without realising, I moved it over to DELETE and pressed hard on the mouse. It was gone, not to Germany, but to the recycle bin.

Oh. Perhaps I'd come back to that one later.

I guess I wanted a few more hours of thinking that he thought I looked like Sarah.

When I'd turned the computer off, I felt quite shaky. For once I decided I wouldn't eat, I'd get a video out instead. I set off for VIDDY VIDDY, our local video rental shop. It's more or less heaven, five minutes from my house. There's a lovely soft carpet and I like sitting on it and just staring at all the films – not even really choosing, but dreaming about them all. They give me time off from myself. I imagine myself as the heroine, or in the landscape, or having all the feelings people have in the films: fear, anger, sadness, happiness; all the feelings I have in real life, but in a different and unexpected order. When I can't choose, I can look at these brilliant boards up on the walls, which list the Top Ten films of the guys who work there. I often choose one of those films, partly so I can chat to them about it.

Those guys are way wicked. They're pretty old, I think at least eighteen, and they must all be students or musicians because they've got lots of hair – not just on their heads, but on their faces. I don't mean old-fashioned beards like my dad's, but little bits of hair in odd places, like on their cheeks or under their noses. It must be dead cool; or maybe they're just short-sighted and miss bits out when they shave.

They're all really into films, because they've seen everything in the shop – or that's what it seems like. If you ask them if they've got something, they say things like: 'Sure. And you could go for the midweek offer and get the sequel, the musical and the Icelandic version – interesting takes on the story.' It could be really snotty and even a bit teachery. But I'm usually so busy working out what they've done with their hair, I just nod and get what they suggest. It's always good.

When I went this time, I had a really big shock. None of the hairy guys were there. Instead there was just one guy without any facial hair, which was a good thing because his face was so totally perfect I didn't want any of it to be covered. He was a bit younger than the others, and he was dark – but not a total 'tall, dark, handsome' stereotype because he was a bit short. Who cares? I'm quite short too – and that's only a problem because I'm quite fat, so all in all, I look quite square.

He was putting videos away behind the counter and was concentrating quite hard, so I could have a good look at him without being noticed. The more I looked, the better he got. Nice shirt, blue eyes, long eyelashes (which I think look better on boys than girls). I didn't look for too long and I didn't think he'd seen me looking – but he suddenly said, 'Can I help you?' without turning round, so maybe he knew I was there.

He had a nice voice too, but as I listened to it, I made an important decision: I wasn't going to let him know that I already had a 'thing' about him. I was going to act cool and mature, so I just casually asked for the film I wanted.

'Yup. I'll get it for you,' he replied, equally casually. He turned away from the counter to get it from the shelves. He even looked nice from behind. He gave me the video; I gave him my card; he typed my details into the computer; I said, 'Thanks,' and left the shop. All ever so casual. I was so pleased with myself, I did a little run along the shopping parade. Then I heard footsteps thudding behind me. It was him. I'd forgotten to pay.

Once I'd got over that embarrassment, which took a large ice cream and a walk round the block, I went home to watch the film. Then came the big decision: how long before I could take it back? If I took it straight away it might look really obvious I wanted to see him again. On the other hand it might look like I was a film lover, which I am. In the end I managed to leave it half an hour after the end of the film. I didn't want to leave it any longer because he might have finished work.

He was still there! He was lovingly cleaning a CD and chatting to the guy there who's got his hair in bunches. I wandered around the comedy section, the drama section and the teen section. I wasn't going near the children's section, even though there are quite a few films in there I like. I couldn't find anything I wanted. I'd either seen them, or wasn't allowed them (I pretend Mum and Dad won't let me watch eighteens but actually it's because I'm too scared), or didn't want to be seen taking them out.

'You could try one of my All Time Top Ten,' came a voice from behind the counter which I knew was his.

I didn't even look up because I knew I would end up blushing. Keeping my head down, I swivelled round to the list of Top Tens. I stared at it, wondering which one was his.

'Owen,' he said softly, just to me. His voice went right through me. I hoped he couldn't tell. I stared at the list but I couldn't make sense of it. I was overcome by finding out his name.

He helped me out. 'How about this?' he said gently, handing me a film. I couldn't stand the tension any more. I marched over to the counter and slammed down my membership card. 'I'll take that as a yes,' he said, with a winning smile.

I did remember to pay this time, but I completely forgot the film.

SIX

From: The boy with the photo
Sent: 20 Feb 3.15 p.m.
To: The girl in the photo
Subject: Nice to see you

Hi Charlie

I'm talking to you. That means I'm looking at your photo while I write. I've put it next to the screen, so I think you are looking at me too.

I did not think I had an idea what you look like when I was writing to you before, but now I think I did have an idea and that idea was that you are something like I thought you would be.

You are just right. Your face fits how you
sound when you write. Of course it does:
it's yours.
You are smiling at me and that's nice. I
will not say any more on this subject
because then you will think I am soft and
sweet and that is not always a good thing
for a boy to be, especially if his friends find
out!
So I will write about something else now.
We were learning about London today
and our teacher told us that men in
dresses look after the castle. Is this true?
I have to go. Schiller just brought me a
lead, which means it is time for him to
take me for a walk.
Your
Frank

I've done it – I thought – I've really done it
now. I had sent the photo days ago, but now
the miserable bomb had exploded. I'd been
sent the loveliest letter of my life: you could
almost call it a love letter, if you read it
carefully and made a few extra things up – but

it wasn't to me, it was to Sarah. He liked me to write to and joke around with, but now he'd got her photo, he'd gone all soppy.

I didn't think I could write to him any more. There was a total gap between the me that wrote the words and the photo he'd got in front of him. Whatever happened, I'd have to tell him what I'd done. I couldn't let him go on thinking that's what I look like. But… but, but, but… there was a bit of me – quite a big bit of me – that wished he *could* go on thinking I look like that, because that's what I *wish* I looked like…

I felt so overwhelmed by all these feelings that I knew there was only one thing to do: eat something. Popcorn popped into my mind, but no sooner was it lodged there, like a stubborn splinter, than I realised it was an edible excuse. It was true that I did want some popcorn, but I also wanted to go to VIDDY VIDDY. That made me feel all emotional again. What was going on? Two months ago I had never been out with a boy. Now, even though I still hadn't actually been out with a boy, I had one who was half in love with me – or rather I was half of the person he was in love with – and another one who seemed to be flirting his socks off, although I'd never actually seen them come off his feet, so maybe he was just being friendly.

I set off up the road to VIDDY VIDDY, trying to decide which film and which flavour popcorn I'd have, although really I was just wishing he'd be there. I managed to decide on the popcorn at the same time.

'Hi,' he said, as I came in. He was there! He was saying hello to me! He remembered me! And he was saying hello!

'Hi,' I said, weakly.

'What did you think of the last film?' he asked, casually.

'Great,' I said. 'I liked all the devices the boy had in his room to keep his brother out.'

'Yeah,' he said. 'It was groundbreaking in its genre.'

'I'd like a device to keep my brothers out of my room, but I can't get a gun licence.'

He laughed. He actually laughed at something I'd said. I couldn't have been happier if I'd have lost five kilos in a week.

'Have you got another one by the same director?' I asked.

'So you're following his work?'

'Yeah. To be honest, the first one of his I took out because of the cover, but now I look for his name.'

'Cool,' he said.

Wow – I had his total approval.

'How about this one next?' he said, picking out a film from one of the racks and handing it to me. His hand brushed my little finger as he gave it to me. Accidentally or deliberately? I could ponder that one for days.

'OK,' I said, when I actually wanted to scream: 'YOU TOUCHED ME!!!'

That was the end of the conversation, apart from, 'Three quid, please,' which he said after I'd shown my card. I managed to pay and remember my card *and* the film. I didn't ask for popcorn: I didn't want him to think I was greedy, although of course he could tell I was by looking at me.

I walked away from the counter and heard: 'Bye, Charlie,' from behind me.

I managed: 'Bye, Owen,' before I got out

of the door and practically fainted.

He had called me by my name! He must have seen it on the card! And I had called him by his name! I had seen it on the board!

Being me, I couldn't just enjoy this attention I was getting from Owen. I had to pick away at it, like my brothers do with the scabs on their knees. Why was he doing it? Was it really because he liked me?

I did what I always do when I have a problem: I told Sarah about it. 'A problem shared is a problem halved' – that's what Mum always says when she wants me to confide in her. That's not true. A problem shared is a problem doubled if you tell Mum, because she always tries to help and makes things worse. If I tell Sarah it's not halved either: it's quartered or sixthed, or eighthed, because she always helps so much, without even trying very hard.

I decided I'd tell her on the way to school. The stretch we walk together is just long enough for me to tell her the problem, and then Hannah and Alice join us and we stop talking about it. Then Sarah thinks about it all day, except when she's using compasses or taking penalties, because you have to concentrate for those. On the way home, she tells me what to do.

I really wanted to tell her about Frank as well, but there was one thing stopping me: the fear that she would ditch me as a friend. It was only one thing, but quite a big one. So I put all that to the back of my mind (which unfortunately is very near the front) and recounted every moment of the Owen episode. I sighed dramatically to indicate how serious the problem was. Amazingly, Sarah let me down enormously because she didn't immediately see what the problem was.

'So this guy, Owen, is friendly and talks about films?'

'Yes,' I sighed, wearily this time. If you're going to sigh more than once, you've got to change the tone of your sigh or people lose interest, I find.

'So what's the problem?'

'THAT IS!' I screeched, so loud that a passing boy on a bike was caused to swerve. 'I don't know what it means! Does he *like* me, in which case I can escalate the intimacy, or is he like that with everyone?'

'Do *you* like him?'

'Don't be daft.'

'You don't?'

'I DOOOO!!' I screeched. Was she being deliberately slow, or was she on some kind of bet to see if she could make me shout three times before I reached the school gates?

It was too late to say any more. We had reached the roundabout; Hannah and Alice bounced up to us, already laughing. Alice thrust her chest at us: she had a new badge. It said: *If you can read this you're too near.*

'I could do with one of those,' I muttered, glancing down at my ballooning boobs, 'except I'd be too embarrassed if anyone came near enough to actually read it.'

Sarah and I weren't alone again until the walk home from school. 'Well,' said Sarah, as confident as Palace's manager before they lose. 'There's only one way to find out.'

'I'm not asking him, or flirting with him, or writing to him, or ringing him up, or sending an email, or buying him a present, or dropping

66

something on the floor by pretend-mistake.'

'None of these are necessary,' she pronounced. 'We will do a controlled experiment.'

We decided that we would replicate the circumstances of me asking for films, only with Sarah standing in for me. Not like she'd stood in for me in the photo to Frank, of course – she would just be a girl like me, but a lot thinner and prettier, taking out a film. If he got chatting, he clearly chats with everyone; if he didn't, then there was clearly something going on between him and me. It was totally scientific.

I couldn't wait any longer to find out this information which would confirm or deny my lifelong happiness, so we went home via VIDDY VIDDY. I waited round the corner outside the sweetshop.

Three sour cola bottle chewies later, she was back. She looked kind of flushed and smiley. My heart sank. Had our plan gone against me and now he had fallen for her? I hadn't thought of that.

I grabbed her by the hands and looked

intensely into her eyes, like they do in films.

'I asked for the film, like you said,' she said.

'Yes,' I said breathlessly, because it seemed to fit the mood of the moment.

'And he got it and said, "We don't get asked for this very often: are you a friend of Charlie's?"' I was just breathless at that. I didn't say anything. She went on: 'So I said "Yes" and then he said, "Tell her to come and see me soon."'

The experiment had been a total success. I almost felt like writing it up and giving it to my science teacher. Even though it didn't involve batteries and circuits, it had conclusively proved its objective. I gave Sarah what was left of the sweets I'd bought for her and we walked back, contentedly chewing.

Well, almost contentedly; I couldn't help thinking about Frank and the mess I'd made by sending him Sarah's photo. If Owen liked me for how I really looked, then maybe Frank would too; but then I could end up with two boyfriends and that would be far too many, especially after having never ever had any. That got me worrying about never having had a boyfriend and what I would do if I suddenly got one. What would we do, what would we talk about, and most of all, what would I wear? Even though one potential boyfriend lived in Germany and the other had already seen me in my tracksuit, I managed to worry about it all the way home.

SEVEN

Before I had total knowledge that Owen was interested in me, I hadn't thought much about what I wore when I went to the shop. It was the usual joggers and baggy T-shirts, long skirts and big jumpers, and of course the mammoth cardigan. All that had to change, but of course not too much, because I didn't want him to guess that I knew his innermost feelings.

I also had a huge internal debate about whether I should go on a diet before I went back to the shop. Sarah and I decided that I should leave a little time, but not too much, before I went in. If I went too soon it would look suspicious and too keen; if I left it too long he might get another girlfriend. We agreed that half a day was about right. Even if I ate nothing at all, I wasn't going to lose anything in that time, so I decided I would eat normally and dress cleverly. I actually ate a bit more than I normally do because I was so nervous.

As for dressing cleverly, I was as clever as I could be within the limitations of my size, my clothes and my time limit. As discussed, I couldn't change my size and the time limit, and I couldn't really do anything about my clothes, because it would make Mum suspicious and I would have to confess I was going out with an older man. As it was, she nearly rumbled me.

I don't know how she guessed. All I did was have a long bath, hair wash, face pack; iron my clothes, borrow some of her jewellery and spend three hours getting ready. OK, I don't normally do that when I'm going to get a viddy, but pre-teens are supposed to be unpredictable, aren't they?

She hovered in the doorway of my room while I was doing my hair for the sixth time.

'Where are you going?' she said, like a police officer.

'To the video shop.'

'What for?'

'I know it sounds weird, but I'm going to get a video.'

'And?'

'Some popcorn.'

She didn't look convinced, and nor was I, but I didn't have time to worry about it. I had to get to the shop by 10.17, which Sarah and I had decided was the best time for the shop to be empty and suitable for a scene of hot romance.

I almost ran to the shop. I looked back and scoffed at my pre-Owen self, plodding along, trying to decide what film to take out. Now it was a different story. I didn't have to be prepared. I could decide what I wanted when I went in. I could browse. I could discuss my film choice with Owen. In the ten minutes it took me to walk to VIDDY VIDDY, I had inflated a brief film discussion into a fully-fledged date in the cinema – complete with popcorn, holding hands and post-credits long, lingering kiss. It would have to be post-credits because we're both so interested in films we have to see who did Johnny Depp's hair, even if he acted someone bald.

I strolled into the shop, trying to look comfortable and relaxed.

'Hi, Charlie,' said Owen, taking the lead. 'You got the message, then?'

'Yup,' I said, incredibly casually, even glancing at the bargain bin as if I were vaguely interested in buying a film. My apparently nonchalant interest must have driven him crazy with passion, because the next thing he said was more or less a proposal of marriage.

'Maybe we could go for a coffee one day, there's something I'd like to talk to you about...'

'Yeah,' I said, still staring at the bargain bin because I felt that if I didn't keep focused on something other than what was actually happening, I might disappear completely into a cloud of over-excitement.

Maybe he actually thought I was interested in the films because he didn't immediately say anything, so I took the lead: 'Now?' – which perhaps seemed a bit uncool. He smiled.

'I can't now. I'm working.'

'Oh yeah,' I managed.

'How about Saturday?'

'OK,' I said, playing safe and trying not to say anything else uncool.

'Ten? Here?'

'OK,' I said again, as it seemed to have gone well last time.

'Great.'

I had to leave after that. I was overwhelmed. Maybe it looked quite cool. Or maybe it looked totally pathetic because I hadn't even attempted to take a video out, so it was completely obvious that I'd only gone in to talk to Owen. The only alternative was that I'd gone in to get a film out, but Owen's more or less proposition of a date had emptied my mind of intelligent thought. Not very impressive.

But there was no denying the proposition. There I was, twelve years old, standing in the middle of the pavement (I had to stand still to register the full impact of this moment), the object of interest of a fit, film-loving boy. I might as well skip GCSEs and marry him now.

Then I gave myself a talking-to, but not out loud. It was, after all, only a proposition of a coffee, at this stage. We must take it one stage at a time. Maybe we'd get married at the end of the week.

No! I had to grow up and stop imagining everything leaping ahead so far and so fast. I found myself walking in the direction of Sarah's house. I had decided to dissipate the excitement by telling someone about it, and it wouldn't be safe to tell anyone in my house for a whole host of reasons I couldn't begin to list. Safe to say, though, that they all involved acute embarrassment.

Sarah's mum answered the door. She was wearing a long flowing dress and had a wig of dark hair that was almost as long as the dress.

'Arwen?' I said, totally unphased.

Her name's actually Sue, but I guessed the costume was Arwen from Lord of the Rings.

'Exactly,' she replied excitedly. 'We've got a whole Lord of the Rings set just come in.'

Sarah's parents have a fancy dress shop. I'm sure lots of people who have fancy dress shops don't actually dress up as a *hobby*. They probably spend their free time carpet-bowling or making felt dachsunds: anything that gets them away from fake blood and skeleton outfits. Not only do Sarah's parents dress up while they're serving in the shop, they sometimes bring costumes home and try them on in the evenings.

'You'd make a great Eowyn,' she said, looking at me dreamily.

'Thanks,' I said, matter of fact for once.

'It's a lovely long, flowing dress—' she started, with a sweeping movement around her knees.

'Great,' I said quickly, 'but I've come to see Sarah.'

'Of course,' she said, with an artistic gesture towards the stairs. I raced up. I don't think she thought I was rude because she knows she's a bit mad.

I burst into Sarah's room, where she was actually doing some homework, and blurted everything out, every word, with all the 'he saids' and 'I saids' and even the bit about looking in the bargain bin. She followed everything with a wide-eyed smiling expression and then leapt on me with a huge hug.

'I'm so pleased for you,' she muttered, as she squeezed me tight.

'So am I.'

Then she pulled away from me and asked the fatal question that ruined it all.

'Are you going to tell your mum?' she asked, looking at me inquisitively with her wide blue eyes.

My world crashed around me – oh, that's a ridiculous thing to say. If I'd broken my back, or my house had been flooded, or my parents had died, my world *would* have crashed around me; but all that had happened was that I'd finally admitted to myself that Owen was a lot older than me and my parents probably wouldn't let me go out with him.

'Tell them what?' I asked, as if I didn't know exactly what.

'That he's sixteen.'

'Sixteen! He's not sixteen!' I gasped. I wasn't that shocked really. I'd thought he was probably sixteen, but hearing the age out loud made it sound older than if I'd just thought it in my head.

'Well, how old is he then?'

'I don't know.'

'Well he must be sixteen, to work in that shop,' she said, very accurately.

'So?'

'So, you know...'

'So, you know what?'

'So you know what your mum will say.'

'No I don't, because she's not going to find out.'

It was Sarah's turn to gasp.

'Well it's only a coffee – at this stage,' I pointed out.

It didn't take long to get her to agree with me. She even offered to cover for me if Mum tried to find out where I was when I was having this coffee of coffees.

Actually I don't like coffee, but I knew I might have to pretend to like it to prove myself older than my years. What if it made me sick? That would be awful. Maybe I could train myself to like coffee in the days leading up to the date, as I now liked to call it. Only trouble with that, my mum might suspect something if I suddenly started asking for a latte in the morning. I decided I might have to risk him thinking I'm a bit of a baby and ask for a Coke instead.

I left Sarah's full of heavy thoughts, but not ones about my weight. I thought it through on the way home, as well as thinking my way through my entire wardrobe, trying to decide what to wear for the 'coffee date'. By the time I got back to my front door I had gone back to my original plan: I wouldn't tell Mum. I was going to be in charge of my life for once.

I turned on the computer to do my homework. There was a mail waiting for me. Even though Owen didn't have my email address and there was no way on earth he could get hold of it, I still somehow dreamt it was from him.

But it was from Frank.

From:	The Visitor
Sent:	2 March 6.24 p.m.
To:	The Visited
Subject:	VISIT!

Hello Charlie

Today I will not tell you about how Schiller has made friends with a girl-dog in the park and is now to be a father. I have better news. Today our teacher told us we will have a visit to London. This is very exciting, isn't it? At last I will see the girl in the photo.

Your excited

Frank

My excited Frank? His panic-stricken Charlie. What could I do? He's going to come and visit!

EIGHT

'Yes,' said Miss Longbottom to our giggling, shuffling, twitching, belching and badly-dressed class. 'There's a possibility of a group exchange.'

Possibility! Only a possibility! Hooray and halleluia: only a possibility! The murmurs of interest and enthusiasm in the class worried me: it felt like everyone was quite keen, but I consoled myself with the thought that even if the entire German class did the exchange, no one could force me to join in.

'It's quite short notice – the suggestion is Easter, so I've done a letter for you to take home. Please bring the reply slips back by the end of the week if you possibly can.'

If I possibly can, I won't. While the sheets were being handed out, I was planning my strategy. It was quite simple, really: I wouldn't give the letter to my mum, and she need never know about the exchange. Perfect. As the letter came into my hands I realised it wasn't perfect at all, because the details of the dates and the arrangements and the possible return visit made me feel all excited. I would love to meet Frank and have him to stay, but I knew I couldn't face up to telling him about the stupid photo business, and I also couldn't imagine him being around when I might just be going out with Owen. It was simpler never to meet him at all.

Perhaps I shouldn't make plans and then they couldn't go wrong. I was so careful: I didn't put the letter in the recycling bin at school because I thought it might be found by a nosey teacher or a goody-goody pupil. I posted it into a recycling bin on the way home and it slipped down, in among the newspapers and the unwanted catalogues and the overwhelming pizza delivery menus.

At home I was relaxed and casual; I even told Mum about the new hockey pitch markings on the playing field so she wouldn't think I was holding anything back. It was all going so well.

I wish Mum hadn't gone swimming. She will insist on going swimming on Ladies' Swim Night. None of the ladies swim much; they hang about at either end of the pool, chatting, and then swim a bit, still chatting, and then get to the other end and chat some more.

When Mum came back from swimming I was writing a mail to Frank, telling him that sadly we wouldn't be able to do the exchange because we hadn't got room to put him up. Then Mum burst in, barely giving me a chance to close the draft before she saw what I'd written.

'I've just seen Hannah's mum at the pool,' she announced. I knew immediately what had happened, but I played it cool.

'Oh yeah,' I said, vaguely.

'She says there's going to be a German exchange'.

'Maybe...'

'What do you mean, maybe?'

'Only if everyone wants to do it.'

'Of course everyone'll want to do it,' she said, bashing on, as Dad calls it. 'Where's the letter?'

'What letter?' I replied, playing it perhaps a bit too cool because that irritated her.

'The letter you were given at school today to give to me.' She enunciated every syllable.

'I've lost it,' I lied, and of course she caught me out.

'So you *did* know about it,' she said, with a reprimanding look. 'I'll ring school in the morning.' She made for the door. I panicked.

'What are you going to say?'

'That we're on for it.'

'No we're not.'

'Of course we are. It'll be lovely, having a German boy to stay.'

'No it won't.'

'Why not?'

'Because we haven't got room for him, and he's a boy, and I don't know if I like him, and I'm shy, and I'm busy, and I don't want to go back there because I'm too young and I'll be homesick and my German isn't good enough, and I don't know if his English is good enough and we might not understand him, and he might get homesick and go back early and it'll all have been a waste of time and money.'

She came right up to me and let forth. 'Yes we have, who cares, I'm sure you like him, you're not shy, or busy, we'll cross that bridge when we come to it, his English is probably excellent, he can ring home, he won't need to, nothing is a waste of time, and we're not paying,' she answered back triumphantly. It was an impressive retort but I wasn't going to admit it.

'You didn't say what we'd do if we can't understand him,' I quibbled.

'Sign language,' she said, sticking out her tongue. 'I'll ring school tomorrow and say yes,' she said as she left.

I turned back to the computer and reluctantly deleted all my excuses to Frank. I would have to write another mail, saying how pleased I was that he was coming over. I couldn't face it now; I'd do it when I could mean at least some of what I was writing.

I went to bed early because there was nothing to do except sleep or eat biscuits. Maybe if I could at least lose a few kilos before Frank came I would be a bit thinner, even if I still didn't look like Sarah. It would no doubt encourage Owen, too. Even if he were mad enough to like me as I was, he would surely like me more if there were less of me. As I lay in bed not going to sleep, this sliver of an idea turned into a big slice of my life. I was going to diet from first thing tomorrow morning up until the moment of Frank's arrival. I did the sums in my head: I had fifty days until the Germans arrived. I had seven kilos to lose, so I had to lose a kilo a week for seven weeks and then I'd have one day left over to go shopping for the new me. I felt really excited about my new plan: so excited I got out of bed and sneaked down for a couple of biscuits because I wouldn't be having any more for forty-nine days.

Next day on the daily walk to school I told Sarah my plan. She did not respond with the support and enthusiasm I expected of her.

'You're not dieting,' she said sniffily.

What was wrong with everyone? At last I was doing something to stop myself looking quite so gross and now no one wanted me to be doing it.

'No, I'm not dieting, as such, I'm just cutting down on popcorn,' I said.

'That's dieting,' she said. 'Any attempt to control your eating and deny the foods you like is dieting.'

'Since when are you such an expert?' I said, as sniffily as she had been to me. 'Besides, it's just healthy eating.'

'I've read about it in magazines.'

'Well, I've read about diets in magazines.'

'So how come your magazines are right and my magazines are wrong?'

'There are more magazines with diets in,' I pointed out.

'Yes, and have you seen all the advertising in between? Low-fat this, no-sugar that. Diets make money, not sense.'

I was beginning to feel I agreed with her. I was also feeling a bit desperate.

'*Some* people lose weight on diets.'

'Only a tiny percentage.'

'Well, why can't I be one of them?'

'What's the point? You'll probably lose it anyway in a couple of years.'

'But I've only got fifty days!'

'Why have you got to change yourself for Frank?'

'I'm not changing myself for Frank. I'm changing myself for Owen as well.'

'All right. For Owen then.'

'And Frank.'

'And every man you ever go out with.'

'Or marry.'

She gave me a weary look.

'The point is, you look fine as you are.'

'I don't! I'm a fat blob and Frank'll be totally disappointed. I've got to do something to make me look more like you!'

There. I'd got all heated and I'd let it slip out. Sarah stopped walking and turned to look at me.

'What do you mean: to look more like me?'

'Well, you know I'd like to look more like you. I've told you that before...' Would she buy this feeble excuse? Of course she didn't.

'Why have you got to look like me by the time Frank arrives?' she asked suspiciously.

I actually wanted to tell her now. Tears were welling up and it was only 8.25 a.m. 'Because I sent him a photo of you and pretended it was me!' I blubbed.

'Oh Charlie,' she said affectionately and gave me a hug. 'Why?'

'Because I didn't want him to know what I looked like, because I wanted him to like me, and I knew he wouldn't like me if I sent a photo of me; so at the last minute I sent one of you, and then I wanted to change it, but Mum had sent it, and then I tried to tell him and I couldn't!' Now I'd started I couldn't stop: 'And now he's sort of fallen for me, but it's not me, it's you, and he's coming in fifty days. I tried to stop it happening but I couldn't and now when he finds out he'll hate me even more than if I'd just sent him my photo in the first place! Even though he'll probably hate me, I'll still like him, but I've made a complete mess because now Owen likes me too. I've been greedy, for boys as well as food!'

After all that I just sobbed for a bit. Sarah held me.

'You silly sausage,' she muttered.

'Don't call me a sausage!' I retorted, coming out of the crying. 'They're really high in fats!'

'OK, you nutty noodle.'

'They're OK, if they're not fried,' I said, a little appeased.

We started walking again, but slowly, because we both wanted to get this sorted before we met Hannah and Alice. Sarah told me what I already knew: 'It looks like Owen likes you for what you look like.'

I sniffed, which meant I agreed with her. I didn't want to actually admit she was right.

'You've got to tell Frank the truth, Charlie.'

'I know. I will.' I dried my eyes, as if the matter was closed, but there was one more thing to say: 'Do you want to write to him?'

'Of course not, I don't do German,' she answered.

'I know, but do you want to write to him in English? He'll understand it.'

'Why would I want to do that?'

'Because he likes you. He's got your photo by his computer.'

'But he likes *you*. He's writing to *you*.'

We laughed then. It all seemed so absurd.

'Tell him, Charlie. It'll make you feel better. Then you'll be able to enjoy meeting Owen more.'

'Yeah,' I said. 'I will.'

The diet didn't go too well that day. I felt so turbulent about Frank I had to have dessert. It was only banana and custard but I had seconds of custard. As soon as I got home I went upstairs to my computer. I just took a banana, because I felt I'd missed the one I hadn't had with the seconds of custard. I wrote and sent the mail before I changed my mind.

From:	The Fibber
Sent:	4 March 4.30 p.m.
To:	The Fibbed
Subject:	The Fib

Dear Frank
I've told you a fib. Well, I sent you a fib.

The photo I sent you is of my best friend,
Sarah. I won't tell you why I sent it. You'll
find out when you arrive.
Until then,
Charlie

There. Done. I felt as if I'd lost something: a
prettier, thinner version of me, as well as the
fun of finding a boy I could talk to like I talk to
a girl, but feel for like I've never felt for a boy
before. Well, before Owen, anyway. Nothing
lasts, I said to myself again, because again, it
hadn't. The only thing that cheered me up was
the thought of my forthcoming date – and I
made a pledge to myself not to fib to Owen,
ever.

NINE

I decided I wouldn't go to much trouble with getting ready for the date, or else Mum would be suspicious and not let me go, so I just did all the things I did last time I went to VIDDY VIDDY, but started earlier. I put my alarm on for 5.30 a.m. so that I'd have at least two hours to get ready before everyone else got up. I couldn't have my bath and hair wash that early in the morning or I'd wake everyone, so I had them the night before. I put the alarm right next to my head on the pillow, so that it would barely ring before I turned it off.

Unfortunately it fell on the floor in the night, so it did ring for a little longer than I'd anticipated in the morning. I scrambled around looking for it and turned it off as quickly as I could. Then I got up and got dressed, which took until about 5.40 a.m. I had one hundred minutes left before I usually get up; I spent those doing my hair. I have never tried out so many styles in one sitting. In fact by the time I'd finished my hair was lank with all the handling it had had. I put it in a ponytail: at least it looked casual, if a little greasy.

I went downstairs looking as relaxed as I could, but Mum immediately rumbled me. 'Where are you off to?' she asked, suspiciously.

'I'm getting a video for tonight,' I said, which may sound completely stupid, but I read in a mag that when you're lying it's better to say something near the truth and then it sounds more probable. It worked. How could she imagine I was off on the first date of my life?

But I was! I felt really light-footed on my way there; I tried not to smile to myself too much because I was worried one of Mum's friends might see me and suspect something.

Once I got in the shop I found I couldn't smile at all because I was so nervous. Owen made it easy for me because he was putting back some videos and barely turned round as he said: 'Hi, Charlie. Shall we go next door?'

'OK,' was all I could say, as if I were a robot.

We walked out of the shop to the café next door, me trying to look as if I did this every day, him looking as if he did, because he did.

'Outside?' he said.

'OK,' I said.

'Coffee?' he said.

'OK' I said, even though, as discussed, I hate coffee.

'Latte?' he said. This sounded a bit sophisticated for me, but I didn't want to admit it.

'OK,' I said, because if you already don't like something, there's no point fussing about exactly how it's made.

I sat down at a table outside, really because I thought if I didn't sit down I might fall over. Owen went into the café to get the coffees. I tried to work out how I'd get round not drinking it. Little did I know how straightforward that would turn out to be. He was back before I'd thought what to do, with two big, blue china cups of steaming coffee, complete with sugar cubes and a little biscuit in a cellophane wrapper. Without thinking I started on the biscuit, to delay the coffee moment. He sat down beautifully, all cross-legged and mature, and smiled at me.

'Like I said, I wanted to ask you something,' said Owen.

Then it happened. The moment to end it all. The apparition at the end of the street: monstrous Mum, looming up behind him.

'OK,' I said, because I really couldn't say anything else.

'As you probably know—' he began, but he didn't get any further. She was upon us.

'Charlie!' she hollered. 'What on earth are you doing?'

'I'm having a coffee,' I said meekly, even though that wasn't entirely true.

Thankfully Owen took control of the situation.

'Hi. I'm Owen. I work in the video shop. You're—'

'Charlie's mum,' she said, before he got the chance.

'Great,' he said, cool as you like. Wasn't he the *least* bit embarrassed to be dating a twelve-year-old? He wasn't, and I soon found out why. 'I'm glad we've met because I wanted to talk to you too.' Did he want to date her as well? *Please!*

'Yes...' said Mum, a bit impatient.

'I'm doing a film module for my Media Studies course...'

I didn't have to hear any more. I couldn't hear any more. Everything came crashing in on me. Owen was still talking, something about 'doing a case study of pre-teen viewing habits'. Pre-teen? How embarrassing. And now all I heard in my head was a big loud voice saying, 'You stupid, STUPID girl.'

It was my own voice. Of course he didn't like me, not big fat me. He just wanted to know what I thought about films.

'I just wanted to know what she thought about films.' There – he'd actually said it.

'Well why couldn't you ask her in the shop?' Mum sounded stern. That got me listening to their terse conversation.

'I'm not allowed to talk about it in the shop. The boss doesn't like it.'

'I'm not surprised,' said Mum, rather seriously. 'She's only twelve.'

'It's only a questionnaire,' said Owen, unfazed. He took a folded sheaf of papers from his pocket and handed them to Mum. 'Maybe you'd like to have a look…'

'Yes,' said Mum, quite nicely, 'and we'll let you know…'

For once I didn't want to kill Mum; I actually felt quite grateful to her. I wanted to get away from there as quickly as possible. Mum said we had to go and I trotted off after her, glad to be out of the situation – although I was also devastated to be out of the situation.

As we crossed the road I glanced back at the café without him seeing, and he was still there, cross-legged and casual, and he was pouring my coffee into his cup. That was all I was to him: a second cup of coffee and a bit of research.

I didn't say anything on the way home, but she started up. 'That was a bit cheeky.'

'Sorry,' I said, thinking she meant me.

'I mean him. He knows how young you are.'

It was so humiliating. I wasn't just stupid and fat, I was young as well.

'He was only asking me questions about films.' Sad, but true.

'Yes, but he asked you out.'

'Yes, but only next door.' Also sad, but true.

'But for a coffee.'

'Only a coffee.'

'Stop defending him.'

She was right. Why was I defending this slimy boy who had promised so much and made me so miserable? I fell silent then and she managed not to talk for a second or two, but then she started up again. 'You don't even like coffee.'

That did it. I stomped off ahead of her until we got home. Then I went straight upstairs and logged on. Why on earth did I do that? I'd made a total mess with Owen, why remind myself I'd made a total mess with Frank as well? I guess I wanted to get all the misery over in one go, before I tried to cheer myself up. There was a mail from Frank.

From: No photo boy
Sent: 7 March 7.24 p.m.
To: Not the girl in the photo
Subject: Where are you?

Hello mystery girl
That was a funny thing to do, but I
understand, I did the same. The photo I
sent you is of my cool friend.
Not really. That *is* me, but where are you?
It is funny for me to write to one girl and
look at another girl. Do you have two
heads? Three eyes? A big spot on your
nose? I am thinking there is something
terrible about you!
Send me a real photo, please.
Tschüss
No photo Frank

If only I did just have two heads, three eyes
and a big spot on my nose! I had something far
more monstrous: those seven stubborn kilos
that I had still not budged. Was there any point
in trying to shift them? He'd probably hate me
for lying even if he liked me for being thin.

Although I noticed he didn't exactly sound furious at my deception, so maybe there was a teeny-weeny bit of light at the end of the long fat tunnel.

Why not keep going with the diet? Well, start again, to be more accurate. Even if I'd blown it with Frank there would presumably be life after the German exchange, and being thinner would cheer me up, if I could just stop myself eating through the misery. I recalculated the days I had left and the amount I could lose. Yes, it was still possible.

But it didn't happen.

I discovered, to my cost, that you can't eat five penguins (the chocolate kind) in an evening and still lose weight, even if you only have half a bowl of cereal the next morning. Ever since I started dieting I seemed to be hungrier – and this was not because I was eating less. Everywhere I looked there seemed to be biscuits saying, 'Eat Me!' Not literally, of course, otherwise I would be hallucinating; but I seemed to notice food more, now that I was supposed to have less.

I wasn't following an official diet because

everyone was so down on that idea, so I simply cut out fat and sugar. But it wasn't that simple. There isn't fat and sugar just in fat and sugar, there's fat and sugar in everything. Did you know there's sugar in chicken and fat in crispbread? If I really did cut out all fat and sugar there'd be nothing left to eat, so I had to eat some, it was just a question of how much. Could I eat breakfast cereal? Of course. Could I eat a scone? Maybe. Could I eat a small portion of ice cream? Unlikely. Could I eat five penguins? Of course not, but I did.

That's another problem: portion size. I knew enough from my pre-dieting days that you can do a lot by controlling portion size. Obviously, a small slice of cake is better for you than a large one, or two. And a teaspoon of ice cream has the same calories as a plate of steamed cauliflower, but that doesn't mean you should always have the ice cream instead of the cauliflower, because once you open the ice cream carton it's never just a teaspoon. Then there is of course the health issue. A plate of cauliflower is much better for you than a teaspoon of ice cream. So are courgettes, beans, oranges, carrots sticks, slices of cucumber, cherry tomatoes and fennel. But they don't make you happy in the same way that ice cream does, except that in the end it doesn't make you happy because it makes you fat.

The situation did not improve in the weeks running up to Frank's arrival. I had failed, I had totally and utterly failed. With one day to go, I had lost a grand total of seven hundred grams. Maybe seven hundred and fifty, if my scales measured fifties. I'd weighed myself with nothing on, I'd weighed myself in the morning, I'd weighed myself without earrings, I'd even cut off some of my hair – but the scales refused to budge. I'd tried the scales in the chemist, when no one was looking. I had to pretend I couldn't decide which toothpaste I wanted until the shop cleared. Even worse, I allowed a generous three kilos for clothes (much as I wanted to weigh less, I couldn't actually bring myself to take my clothes off in the shop), but I still weighed more than at home. I vowed to boycott that shop for ever, or at least until I really did need more toothpaste.

Being fat wasn't something you could ignore, or forget about. It affected every minute of every day because it was always there, reminding you of your greed, your lack of self-control, your inability to use that small but useful little word, 'no'.

All along, I'd hoped I would suddenly manage to do better, so I hadn't sent Frank my real photo. I thought it wouldn't matter when he finally saw me, and at least I'd be thin, even if I wasn't Sarah. As the day of his arrival got nearer and it got clearer that I wasn't going to be any thinner at all, I gave up. Not just dieting, but on the hope that he'd like me. Who ever liked a big fat liar?

I didn't bother to dress up for the arrival. It was at school, so I had to wear uniform anyway, but I could have done something special with my hair or worn invisible mascara. All the German group were really excited all day. Hannah and Alice were giggling away, the boys were all discussing which computer game they were going to play first; I just kept quiet.

Their coach was due at 4.00 p.m., which is

when we finish school. When the bell went, everyone rushed out into the car park. I wandered out behind them. A huge blue-and-white coach with German writing on it was just pulling into the school. As it came to a stop the kids on it got up and looked out of the window, looking for their penfriends.

There was no mistaking Frank: he was even more like his photo than I thought. His hair was very, very dark and it was thick and spiked in all sorts of different directions. His eyes were sparkly green and he was wearing a black T-shirt and faded jeans. As he stepped off the coach I saw he had big, laced boots, only a bit undone.

All the others were greeting their friends. Frank looked around. I'd have to go up to him and say, 'Hi, I'm Charlie. Sorry.' But he came up to me, smiled, and said: 'Hi.'

He had a photo of me in his hand.

TEN

'Where did you get that photo?' I said, rather stroppily – particularly as it was the first thing I said to him.

'Charlie sent it to me.' He had far less of an accent than I'd expected. I thought he'd sound like a German character in a film, but his accent was much softer, like a footballer who's lived here for years.

'But *I'm* Charlie.'

He looked really shocked. 'I thought you were her friend.'

What a start. Everyone else was moving around us. Hannah saying hello to Erica, Alice and Barbara already laughing. Hannah and

Alice were obviously going to pass on their giggling habits.

'Where is Charlie? I want to meet her,' he said, looking around.

'I'm here,' I said, because I was.

'So there isn't another Charlie, the girl who writes to me?'

'No.'

'And you are Charlie, the girl who writes to me?' He looked confused, and I wasn't surprised. I was only just one step ahead.

'So why did you tell me that this photo wasn't you?'

'Because I thought I sent you a different photo.'

We both laughed, then. It was so absurd. Parents were starting to arrive with cars to take the visitors and luggage home. I looked around for Mum – and not just because I wanted a lift. I was beginning to put two and two together, and it looked to me like she was a hot candidate for four.

'Are you not sure what you look like?' he said, teasing.

'Sometimes,' I said. 'I did put my friend's

110

photo in an envelope.' I put on a suspicious detective accent: 'I have reason to suspect that someone interfered with it!'

He laughed. Then Mum appeared, looking a bit flustered.

'Hello, Frank,' she said, shaking hands. 'Sorry I'm late, I couldn't find anyone to look after the triplets. I had to *pay* the neighbour in the end.'

I gave Frank a look. 'You see, I told you they were bad.'

'Could you not bring them here?'

'Not ideally,' she said. 'It's better if you meet them on home territory. Like many wild animals.'

Frank looked worried. 'Do they bite?'

'Only each other's heads off,' said Mum picking up his bag and moving ahead.

'Does that mean yes or no?' asked Frank quietly, as we followed Mum.

'No. It's an English phrase meaning they argue.'

'Oh. I see. I have still a lot to learn.'

I felt quite comfortable with him, even though we'd only just met and had immediately been confronted with the hideous photo situation. He tried to talk about it again in the car.

'So what do you think happened with the photos?'

I glanced at Mum. She caught my eye in the car mirror then carried on looking at the road.

'I have not yet arrested my prime suspect. I will let you know when they are safely behind bars.'

'Is that in a pub?' asked Frank.

'No, it's in prison,' I said darkly.

As soon as we got home the boys leapt on Frank, literally. They showed him the den they'd made for him in their room, complete with arsenal, a selection of torches, and back copies of *Goblin Weekly* – their favourite magazine. Somewhere amongst all the junk was a mattress for him to sleep on. Then they took him into the garden to play football. He had to save one hundred and sixty-three penalties before they let him go.

I took this opportunity to interrogate my prime suspect. She was in the kitchen peeling potatoes, so she had her back to me, but I knew she knew I was there. Her first tactic was deflection.

'He seems like a nice boy.'

'Yes, he is.'

'Looks like you'll have a good time while he's here.'

'Yes, I expect we shall.' I thought I was being very cool with her. 'Despite all the misunderstandings,' I said in an accusing tone.

'Oh, yes...' she said, noncommittally.

I'd had enough then. Why didn't she just admit what she'd done? I blew.

'Why the hell did you put my photo in that envelope?'

She put her peeler down then and turned round. She was quite fierce.

'Because you were going to tell him a silly lie!'

'It wasn't silly to me! I wanted him to like me – and he wouldn't if he knew what I looked like!'

'Well he *did* find out what you look like and he *still* likes you – and I thought that maybe it was about time you realised that you look fine, because no amount of me telling you will make you believe it!' She turned back to the potato peeling. She looked a bit out of breath. She wiped her eye with the back of her hand. Maybe she was even crying?

I didn't know what to say because really I knew she was right, but I couldn't just admit it there and then.

'Do you want help with the potatoes?' I asked.

'No thanks,' she said, quietly.

I went up behind her and gave her a little hug, leaning my head on her back. Then the boys came back in, flung off their trainers, and introduced Frank to our biscuit tin.

Later on, after dinner, when we sat in the lounge and played on the computer, I couldn't help talking about the photo again.

'My mum swapped the photos around. She thought I'd made a mistake.'

'It turned out OK, I think,' he said quietly.

'Yes, I think so.'

We stayed up late, talking about everything under the sun and even more extended areas of the galaxy. We also included an in-depth planning meeting of our visit to central

London the next day. I promised him we'd go to the Tower of London.

'So I get to see the men in skirts?' he said, with interest.

'Yup, and we'll go to Buckingham Palace and see the soldiers in their big, furry hats.'

'I think maybe you have a funny country.'

'Yeah,' I said. 'Good, isn't it?'

Hannah and Alice came to town with us, with their German friends of course; both German girls were really quiet, but maybe they were quiet in German too. Mind you, it was just as well they were quiet because Hannah and Alice were doing their usual shrieking laughter at anything the least bit funny. I explained to Frank that it's their hobby.

We went into town on the train and then walked up to Buckingham Palace. I must say I felt quite proud of my dirty old city. As the train comes into Charing Cross you go over the river and you can see the London Eye, and Big Ben, and the riverboats chugging round the huge sweeping bend in the Thames that you can see from St Paul's in the east down to

Chelsea in the west. I tried to show all this to Frank but it went so fast I was mainly pointing and squeaking.

We walked through St James's Park to the palace. We had a drink, fed the ducks, and even saw a pelican. I felt like I'd really arrived – not just in the park, but in my life. I could have come up to London like this any weekend of the year, but it made it much more special showing it to someone else, like it was in colour instead of black-and-white.

We were just in time for the Changing of the Guard. Now we were all laughing as much as Hannah and Alice, because we couldn't believe the busbies. They looked like large guinea pigs sitting on the soldiers' heads – and the chin straps were also ridiculous: they sat precariously on their chins and didn't look like they held the helmets on. Fat lot of use they'd be if someone did storm the palace. Although if that happened, I expect the guards would scarper and the SAS would parachute down instead.

After the guard had changed, we took a boat down the river and went to the Tower of

London. Frank thought the Beefeaters were even more ridiculous than the guards. We saw the Queen's jewellery and decided it was a bit fancy for most discos; we saw where they cut off Anne Boleyn's head and decided we were glad that it wouldn't happen now if you didn't have a baby boy.

It was when we decided to have an ice cream on Tower Bridge that the strange thing happened and, as far as I can remember, this has never ever happened to me before. Everyone was getting out their money and choosing what they wanted. Usually when I look at the display my mouth waters at the thought of what I'm going to choose, and usually I don't need to choose because I've been thinking about what I'm going to have all morning and I've known what I want for at least the last half hour. This time I looked at the board and I thought about how I felt and something in me clicked into a different gear.

'I'll buy you one. What would you like?' It was Hannah asking me.

'It's OK. I don't really want one.' She looked completely taken aback. I knew why: she had never heard me say those words before. Not about food.

'You don't *want* one?'

'No,' I said simply.

'You're not dieting, are you?' she whispered.

'No,' I said, 'I'm just not hungry.'

It was true. Amazing. Not being hungry hadn't stopped me eating in the past, but now it did.

We stopped on the bridge to look at the boats. Frank stood next to me, his arm right next to mine as we leant on the barrier. I'd noticed he always stood close to me; I didn't mind: I wanted him to get even closer.

He didn't. He didn't that day and he didn't the next few days either. He was still friendly and funny; but he never showed any sign that I was more to him than a chubby English pal. The tubby girl in the scraggy clothes. Yes, I had a good sense of humour, but that didn't make you want to kiss someone, did it? After all, you can't kiss and laugh at the same time.

I had decided we'd stick to the laughter, but as the stay drew to its close, that got harder.

You're supposed to get more relaxed and outgoing as you get to know someone, but Frank did it the other way round. He went in on himself, like a tortoise in a shell. The boys couldn't even get him to have a play fight. I couldn't get him to do anything.

'Do you want to go out?'

'Not really, thank you.'

'Do you want to stay in?'

'Not really, thank you.'

What was wrong with him? It was like his English had got worse. Either that, or he didn't want to talk to me. What had I done? What had I not done? I really didn't know what to do, or not do.

Maybe Mum had noticed, or maybe she was just being her usual annoying self without even trying – whichever it was, she still managed to bring on the crisis. She cheerily told us the bad news, which she thought was really good news: 'Sue's decided to have a *Lord of the Rings* party.'

I groaned inside. What was Sue up to? Was she promoting the new costumes? Had Mum put her up to it? Or did she, amazingly, just want a party? Bearing in mind that Sue loves parties so much she once had a party on a Wednesday to celebrate Wednesdays, perhaps that's all it was: a party for a party's sake.

The boys were really excited: they all wanted to be hobbits. Mum wanted to be Rosie Cotton, Dad wanted to be Gandalf, and I wanted to be anyone whose costume would fit me. But what would Frank be? Miserable, on current evidence.

ELEVEN

Not everyone had my size problems, but everyone had to find something to wear to the party, so we all went down to Sarah's parents' shop. It's like an Aladdin's cave, and does in fact have various styles of Aladdin outfits in it: baby Aladdin, outsize Aladdin and sexy Aladdin, to name but a few. The shop is small and stuffed with costumes, make-up, masks and bleeding body parts (plastic). The *Lord of the Rings* outfits were all in one corner, hanging on a rail. Sarah was the first to choose, of course, and we all knew who she'd be: Arwen the beautiful elven princess. She went to try the dress on, even though it was bound to fit.

My turn. I looked at the rail. Maybe I could be an orc. They're pretty gross and suited how I felt about myself. Unfortunately Sarah's mum didn't have any orc costumes. I looked through all the costumes on the rack, thinking of the films. In this situation I actually realised one positive aspect of living with my brothers: they had forced me to sit through all the films on video, so I actually knew the story and the characters. I picked some clothes for Eowyn, because she's really brave and heroic. Maybe some of those qualities would rub off on me.

I decided not to try the costume on. If it was far too small my mum would be bound to find out, and she'd ring Sarah's mum, and she'd ring the factory and ask them to make a specially huge costume just for me. I didn't want all that attention. I'd see if I could squeeze into the dress back at home, when it was too late to do anything about it being too small.

I was hoping Frank was going to choose Aragorn because he's the handsome hero, but he chose Faramir instead. He said Aragorn was 'too obvious'. Exactly. That's the great thing about him, that he's obviously handsome, heroic and has a great heart, even if his hair is badly in need of a wash. Faramir's the one whose brother gets killed and whose dad goes mad. Not such a hot date.

As if my clothing crisis was not enough, Frank managed to bring on another trauma. After days of not wanting to do anything, he suddenly came up with something to do: 'How about we borrow a video?'

He couldn't have said anything worse. Of course I wanted to watch a video with him, and I was really pleased he had suggested doing something, but the last thing I wanted to do was go to VIDDY VIDDY with him. It didn't help that Mum was in the room when he said it.

'That's a good idea,' she piped. I could have throttled her.

'We haven't got time,' I panicked.

''Course you have,' she riposted. 'You've been on the computer most of the afternoon.'

'And now I have to do my homework,' I lied.

123

'I thought you said you hadn't got any homework while Frank's here.'

That had been a lie too, but it was too late to tell the truth.

'If you don't want to—' Frank started, aware that this was a difficult mother–daughter moment.

'I do,' I found myself saying, as I grabbed my fleece.

I didn't want to see Owen and I didn't want Frank to see Owen. As we took the well-trodden streets to VIDDY VIDDY I made a big birthday cake-type wish that Owen wouldn't be there. Perhaps I should have waited till my birthday: he was.

As soon as we walked in, he looked up from his CD cleaning.

'Hello, Charlie. Long time no film.'

'I've been really busy,' I lied.

'I can see that,' he cheekily replied, nodding at Frank.

I don't know if Frank got embarrassed, but he went round the corner to look at the science fiction section. I browsed the European art house films while my blush faded, which was a bit of a giveaway because I never normally look at them.

'Can I have a word?' called Owen, from the counter.

'Which one?' I quipped.

He beckoned me to the counter. I trotted over to him like an obedient puppy. Frank was still embedded in the *Star Trek* shelf.

Owen leant towards me and quietly said: 'I'm sorry about the other day…'

'That's OK,' I muttered.

His voice fell to a whisper, as if he didn't want anyone to know. 'I think she thought I wanted to ask you out!' Then he did the cruellest thing. He laughed, as if this was the most ridiculous idea in the world. I had to laugh along, otherwise it would look like that was what I thought too, which of course it was. 'I've been meaning to put things straight ever since, but haven't seen you.'

'I've been busy,' I managed to blurt out, repeating myself I know, but at least I'd said something.

'Well, I hope you won't be too busy to help me,' he forged on.

'Probably not,' I said, thinking of my sad life once Frank had gone home.

'Will you help me with this film module?'

'OK,' I said meekly. 'When?'

But I didn't hear his answer, because someone pulled me by the arms. Someone marched me over to the drama section. Someone grabbed me, like in all the best films, and gave me the most fantastic kiss on the mouth.

Thank goodness that someone was Frank.

I couldn't believe it. Not only had he kissed me, but in public, in front of Owen, Keanu Reeves, Will Smith, Madonna and Betty Grable (those last few are on video covers). My only quibble was that the kiss had been extremely short, but I was in no mood to complain.

Owen looked a little surprised and made himself busy behind the counter. I took the opportunity to steer Frank out of the shop, video forgotten.

'Why did you do that?' I said on the way home, which wasn't what I meant to say at all.

'Did you not want me to do that?' he said, looking worried.

'Oh yes, but in the shop…?'

'I was angry with that man. I thought he liked you…'

'You mean you were jealous?'

'Yes.'

'Oh no. I mean, no, no, no! He doesn't like me.' For once I was sure of something.

'Oh,' said Frank, a bit deflated. 'I feel stupid now.'

'Don't feel stupid,' I said. 'That's my job.'

We laughed then. Then he looked serious.

'I wanted to kiss you all week.'

'Why didn't you?'

He looked a bit cross. 'Why didn't *you*? In my country girls kiss boys. In yours too?'

'Yes,' I admitted. 'But I'm a bit shy,' I fibbed, not wanting to go into the whole business about my fat zone.

'So am I,' he retorted. 'And…' He hesitated.

'You've got more excuses?' I teased.

'Yes,' he said without smiling. 'I have a problem.' I felt really worried then. Did he have an illness, a tragedy about to happen? 'I

127

hide it but I know it's there.' Now it sounded less serious. Perhaps a scar, or a wart?

He suddenly lifted his T-shirt. I didn't know what to say. He had a completely normal, scar-free, wart-free chest.

'I am skinny, no?' he said, earnestly.

I wanted to laugh, but I could see that he thought this was a serious problem. Perhaps as serious as I thought my fat was.

'No, you're not,' I said.

'Really?' he said, dropping his T-shirt.

'Really,' I said.

'Oh,' he said, a bit disappointed. 'We could have kissed a few days ago. We have to catch up.'

And he kissed me again. I thought I'd never be able to kiss and think, but now, even on only my second ever kiss, I was thinking that I forgave everyone: Owen for flirting and misleading me, Mum for mixing everything up, Frank for not kissing me, and me, for making such a fuss about everything.

It took us a while to get home. The boys immediately clustered round us, asking if they could watch the film too, and we had to confess that we hadn't got one out. They thought we'd gone mad.

I'd never felt saner. Or more normal. I felt like other people, or what I thought other people felt like. I had a boyfriend and I was going to a party – and that was all I wanted, for now. In the future I wanted peace in the Middle East, to save the Black Rhinoceros and to have my own home cinema, but I supposed they would have to wait.

We spent most of Saturday getting ready. Our family was contributing the elven bread which we had interpreted as filled pitta breads, because the elven bread in the films doesn't look too appetising. Frank and I helped make them while the boys got their feet dirty. Unfortunately Sarah's parents wanted it to be a party for all the families who'd hosted the visit, so the boys and my parents were coming along. The boys were all going as hobbits so they were making their feet dirty and hairy. In the end Mum and Dad were going as elves, so they'd bought Spock ears from the shop.

I had never bothered to try my Eowyn costume on, but it was much easier now that I was in love. My head had grown bigger with my heart and I just assumed I looked good. So perhaps my perceptions were distorted, but I actually thought the costume worked. It went in at the waist, but miraculously wasn't too tight. It was soft and flowing, but not too girly. After all, Eowyn's a gallant fighter too.

Frank looked totally cool as Faramir. Mind you, I'd have thought he'd be totally cool in a bin bag. I still had to tease him.

'Why didn't you choose Aragorn? He's my favourite.'

'Because he doesn't end up with Eowyn.'

'But nor does Faramir.'

'He does in the book.'

Trust me to fall for someone who's actually read *Lord of the Rings*.

Sarah's mum, dressed as Galadriel the Elven Queen, started to organise games. The first was Hunt the Ring. We decided to sit it out. We lounged on the sofa together. I'd always wanted to do that with a boy. He put his arm round my 'waist'.

'I have a question.'

'I may have an answer.'

'I don't know why you tried to send me Sarah's photo.'

I did have an answer, but it was hard to actually say it out loud. I skirted round it.

'Well, she's pretty, and—'

'So are you.'

'Thank you, but' – the 'f' word suddenly popped out – 'I'm too fat.'

He looked at me. 'I don't think you are. I never thought you were. From the day I got your photo.'

I thought about this for a good while. I thought about all the worry, the sadness, the disappointment that he liked the look of Sarah and the sound of me. He didn't. He'd always known what I looked like and he'd always like me. For me. The way I was. The way I am.

I looked at him. He meant it. He really meant it and, for the first time in my life, I believed it.

'You're right. I don't think I'm fat.'

We kissed, while everyone around us was busy laughing and playing games and pretending not to be distracted by our brilliant moment. Then I said what I never thought I'd ever say.

'I've just got big bones.'

AMANDA SWIFT

THE BOYS' CLUB

Joe is twelve and very, very worried about girls. Girls turn boys into dribbling wrecks. They make you sweat and your tummy feel funny. They make you ditch your mates and football practice to go snogging in their bedrooms for hours. Joe knows. He's seen it happen to his brother.

Joe wants none of it. And he doesn't want his friends to change either. So he comes up with the Boys' Club: a top-secret organization where boys can be boys and have nothing to do with girls. But in reality it's a bit more complicated... Because things do change. And, with the arrival of Alex, a new face around school, Joe's life is about to change more than most...

ISBN 0-689-83754-2